MERMAIDS ROCK

The Secret Wreck

To everyone who loves magical underwater worlds
– LC

STRIPES PUBLISHING LIMITED
An imprint of the Little Tiger Group
1 Coda Studios, 189 Munster Road,
London SW6 6AW

Imported into the EEA by Penguin Random House Ireland,
Morrison Chambers, 32 Nassau Street, Dublin D02 YH68

A paperback original
First published in Great Britain in 2021

ISBN: 978-1-78895-414-3

A CIP catalogue record for this book is available from
the British Library.

Printed and bound in the UK.

The Forest Stewardship Council® (FSC®) is a global, not-for-profit organization
dedicated to the promotion of responsible forest management worldwide. FSC defines
standards based on agreed principles for responsible forest stewardship that are supported
by environmental, social, and economic stakeholders. To learn more, visit www.fsc.org

2 4 6 8 10 9 7 5 3 1

MERMAIDS ROCK

The Secret Wreck

Linda Chapman
Illustrated by Mirelle Ortega

LITTLE TIGER
LONDON

Contents

Welcome to Mermaids Rock!

Marina
& Sami

Kai & Tommy

Naya &
Octavia

Coralie & Dash

Luna &
Melly

Chapter One
A *Fin-tastic* Idea

"Come over here, everyone!" said Coralie, clapping her hands and swishing her glittering purple tail. "We need to get on with our play."

It was the school holidays and Coralie had decided that it would be fun if she and the rest of the Save the Sea Creatures gang – Marina, Naya, Kai and Luna – put on a play for their parents at the end of the week. To her delight, her friends had agreed but, since they had arrived near the anemone field that morning, all they'd done was mess around and ignore her calls to get started.

"We don't want to start on the play yet, Coralie!" shouted Marina.

She and Kai were having a competition to see who could turn the most somersaults in the clear turquoise water of the reef.

"We're having fun!" Marina whooped.

Kai turned four somersaults in a row and Marina promptly turned five.

Coralie felt torn. She loved playing games with her friends, and part of her wanted to swim over and join in with the somersault competition, but if they didn't start to rehearse soon the play wasn't going to be ready. She glanced at the others. Naya was engrossed in taking notes as she studied an unusual yellow sea dragon peeping out of a patch of long seagrass. Luna, Coralie's cousin who was a couple of years younger than the rest of them, was making friends with a large blue parrotfish. It was swimming round her, blowing bubbles out of its big mouth.

Luna had a magical way with all animals. She only had to start humming and even the largest sea creature would swim over, wanting to be her friend. It was a useful talent to have!

Coralie frowned. It wasn't just her friends – even the pets weren't listening to her! Dash, Coralie's young bottlenose dolphin, was playing tag with Tommy, Kai's hawksbill turtle. The two of them were swerving through the large branching yellow-and-red sea fans and swooping over the beds of anemones, making shoals of tiny fish scatter out of their way. Octavia, Naya's octopus, was teasing Melly, Luna's gentle manatee, by creeping up behind her and tickling her with her long arms before shooting away in a stream of cheeky bubbles. Marina's little golden seahorse, Sami, bobbed up and down nearby, shaking with laughter as he watched.

Coralie decided enough was enough. "Right, stop it now!" she called, grabbing handfuls of green seaweed and throwing it at her friends. "You need to come here and listen to me or our play is never going to be ready on time!"

The others yelled as the seaweed splatted against them, but they did stop what they were doing and swam over.

"We really should get started," Coralie pleaded. "I know it's the holidays, but doing the play will be fun! We've got to decide what it's going to be about and what everyone's part will be. All we've agreed so far is that I'm directing it," she added with a quick look at Marina.

Marina was usually in charge of anything the gang did. She always came up with great ideas for adventures they could have. *But this play is* my *idea*, thought Coralie. *It's my turn to organize things*. The thought made her feel both excited and nervous. It would be fun to be the boss, but if it went wrong then she would feel that it was her fault. She really wanted this play to be good!

"Can the play be about an animal?" asked Luna eagerly.

"Maybe," said Coralie. "But it has to be an interesting one."

"Ooh, sea slugs are fascinating," Naya said quickly. "Did you know that a sea slug can be both male and female at the same time, and some are as small as grains of sand while others are as big as—"

"Naya!" Coralie interrupted. "Our play is not going to be about sea slugs." She caught Kai's eye and grinned suddenly as she thought of a joke. "Not this *SLIME* anyway!"

Kai high-fived her while the others groaned and Marina splashed her with her tail.

"How about doing a play about famous scientists and their discoveries then?" Naya suggested hopefully.

"Boring!" exclaimed Kai, pushing a hand through his short black hair. "I think we should do a play about something scary like the time we went to the Midnight Zone and that giant squid almost ate Luna."

"That was super exciting," Coralie agreed.

Luna shivered at the memory. "No, let's not do it about that. I don't want to think about it!" She hugged Melly who nuzzled against her. Melly was the largest of the pets, but she was also the gentlest. She had a round grey body, a large nose and tiny, kindly dark eyes.

"I also think the play should be about something exciting," said Marina. Sami nodded as he bobbed round her head. He always agreed with Marina. "How about we do a play where we race to the Atlantic Ocean to rescue sea birds after an oil spill?" she suggested. "Or one about going to the Great Barrier Reef to stop a shoal of crown-of-thorns starfish destroying the coral there or—"

"Yes, yes, we could do something like that," Coralie interrupted. She actually liked both those ideas, but she didn't want to do something Marina had thought up. This was *her* play. "It should definitely be an exciting play with lots of danger in it." She gasped. "I know! Why don't we do a play about humans?"

"Humans aren't dangerous," said Marina, frowning.

"Yes they are," said Coralie. "They catch sea creatures, they destroy coral reefs with their fishing boats and spill oil into the sea…"

"And they hurt sea creatures like whales," said Luna, her eyes wide. "When my mum had just started working at the Marine Sanctuary, she helped a young humpback whale that had been injured by humans. She met him in the Red Sea near a shipwreck. He had a wound from a harpoon gun so Mum brought him back to our sanctuary. I called him Wally and he was so friendly! It took Mum ages to heal him but, when he was better, she made sure he got safely back to his home."

"See," Coralie said triumphantly to Marina. "If it wasn't for Auntie Erin, Wally could have been in real trouble."

"Not all humans are dangerous though," Marina argued. "Some of them really care about the oceans."

"No they don't," said Coralie.

"Yes they do!" Marina insisted. "I've been to lots of places with my dad where I've seen humans helping sea creatures."

Marina's dad was a marine scientist and before she had come to live at Mermaids Rock she had travelled all round the world with him while he did his research. "There are human organizations that protect the oceans and look after sea creatures, and I've seen them helping to clear up after disasters just like we do."

Coralie gave a disbelieving sniff. "Well, maybe there are a *few* humans like that, but most of them are dangerous."

"No they're not!" Marina said, swishing her tail at Coralie in frustration. "Naya, you agree with me, don't you? You know humans aren't all bad."

"Um… Well…" Naya looked from one to the other, clearly not wanting to take sides.

"I don't like humans because they hurt Wally the whale," declared Luna.

"I think they are pretty dangerous, Marina," said Kai.

"You're all being totally *squid-iculous*!"

Marina exclaimed.

Their voices rose as they argued.

"Quiet!" Coralie shouted. They all looked at her. "OK, I've made my decision. We will do an exciting and *scary* play about humans." She saw Marina open her mouth and hurried on before she could be interrupted. "We'll use today to do some research. We'll find out more about humans and then tomorrow we can decide exactly what the play will be about."

"Ooh, research – yay!" Naya said happily. "I've got some books about humans at home. We could use those and we could borrow some of Marina's dad's books too."

Coralie hesitated. Doing research by reading books sounded far too much like a school project for her liking. "Or we could also speak to merpeople who know about humans," she said. "Glenda's mum used to study them, didn't she?"

Glenda Seaglass was in their class at school.

Her strict father, Razeem, was Chief of the Merguards, the group of merpeople who protected their remote coral reef. "Why don't we go and talk to her?"

"We can't. Glenda's family have gone away on holiday this week," said Kai. "Chief Razeem put my mum in charge of the merguards until he gets back."

Marina gasped. "If Chief Razeem is away, maybe your mum would let us use the whirlpool to travel somewhere to do some *real* research on humans, Kai!"

Kai's face lit up. "You mean go on another adventure? That would be *clam-tastic*!"

"But we're not allowed to go near humans, remember," Naya said.

Coralie thought fast. She loved the idea of having a new adventure but she also knew that there was no way Kai's mum would agree to them going somewhere that was close to humans. The merpeople had a rule to never let humans see them – to keep their homes and lives secret and safe. So, what could they do? Surely there was an adventure they could go on… Something Luna had said earlier popped into Coralie's brain.

"I've got it!" she exclaimed. "We don't have to go somewhere where humans actually *are* to find out more about them. We can go to where humans *were*."

The others looked confused.

"What do you mean?" Marina demanded.

Coralie's eyes sparkled. "Luna said Auntie Erin found the injured whale near a shipwreck. Well, shipwrecks are full of human objects, aren't they? I bet we could discover loads about humans if we went to the Red Sea and found a shipwreck to explore."

Marina clapped. "That's a *krill-iant* idea!"

"*Spray-mazing!*" said Kai, turning a somersault with Tommy.

"Oh yes," breathed Naya, grabbing two of Octavia's arms and dancing round with her. "We'd be like real researchers doing a proper scientific investigation!"

"And it would be safe," said Luna, "because there wouldn't be any actual humans on a wreck."

"The Red Sea isn't that safe," Marina pointed out. "I've been there once before with my dad. If we go there, we'll have to watch out for tiger sharks. There are also dangerous fish, like scorpionfish and surgeonfish, and fish that will attack you if you go too close to their nest, like titan triggerfish, and—"

"But it'll be a *fin-tastic* adventure!" Coralie interrupted quickly as she saw Luna's eyes widen in alarm.

Kai nodded. "It definitely will!" he said gleefully. "Let's go and ask Mum right away!"

Chapter Two
Off on a New Adventure

Indra, Kai's mum, was patrolling by Mermaids Rock – a huge submerged rock shaped like a mermaid's tail that marked the entrance to the merpeople's realm. Around the base of the rock there was a spinning whirlpool that linked to a network of other small whirlpools all around the world. If a merperson said the name of the place they wanted to go to and dived into the whirlpool, they were transported to their destination by magic.

The merpeople used the whirlpool to go

and help out whenever there was a natural or man-made disaster. They also used it to travel for research and to rescue sea creatures in distress. Merchildren were not supposed to use the whirlpool without permission – although Coralie and her friends had broken that rule quite a few times since Marina had come to live at Mermaids Rock!

Indra was holding her long, sharp trident, her dark hair tied back in a neat bun. She was swimming with another merguard – a bearded merman called Rohan – and they were watching the vast expanse of sea beyond Mermaids Rock. The lived in a very isolated part of the ocean but the guards had to keep a close eye out for dangerous creatures like orcas or great white sharks – anything that might threaten the merpeople or the beautiful reef. Fortunately, humans very rarely came anywhere near.

The gang swooshed to a stop beside

the guards. "Mum! Mum! Can we use the whirlpool?" Kai burst out.

Indra's eyebrows rose in surprise. "Use the whirlpool? Why?"

Kai, Marina, Naya and Coralie talked over each other as they all tried to explain.

"Whoa! Whoa!" Indra said, lifting up her trident for quiet. "So, let me get this straight: you want to go and do some research about humans on a shipwreck?"

"Yes, we want to go to the Red Sea," said Marina eagerly. "There are lots of shipwrecks there."

"Please say we can, please, Mum," begged Kai. "We'll stay well away from any humans."

Coralie crossed her fingers, while Indra considered it.

"OK," Indra said finally. "You'll need to ask your parents' permission first, but if they say yes then you can go."

The older ones all whooped and cheered though Luna still looked a bit anxious. Coralie hugged her. "Don't worry," she told her cousin. "I promise I'll look after you."

Melly nudged Luna with her nose as if to say, "Me too!"

"But you need to take a first-aid kit with you and you must be back by teatime," said Indra. "If you're not back by then, I will come and find you – and I can tell you now I won't be happy if I have to do that!"

"Thanks, Mum, you're the best!" said Kai, hugging her. "And we'll *dolphin-itely* make sure we're back by teatime."

"I'll go and get the first-aid kit now," said Marina. "I can borrow one from my dad."

"I'll collect some other things too," said Naya. "I'll bring some of my inventions – lanterns for all of us, healing paste and phosphorescent paint in case we're somewhere dark and need to mark our way. Oh, and a notebook so we can write down our findings!"

"I'll bring snacks," said Kai. "Adventures always need snacks."

Coralie nodded in agreement.

"Let's meet back here in twenty minutes," Marina exclaimed. "Prepared for adventure and ready to go!"

A little while later, they gathered at the whirlpool with their seaweed bags slung over their shoulders. Naya's was the biggest. She liked to be prepared for anything!

"This is going to be so much fun!" Coralie whispered to Dash. He whistled and clapped his fins in excitement. Like all the other pets, he could understand what was said to him, but couldn't answer back, at least not in merpeople language.

"Now, remember what I said," Indra warned them. "You must be back by teatime or I *will* come looking for you."

"Don't worry, Indra," said Marina. "I'll have us all safely home by then."

"So will I," said Coralie quickly. After all, the adventure had been her idea and she didn't want Marina taking charge.

"When you're in the Red Sea, make sure you only go to wrecks that are deep down," said Rohan, rubbing his long beard.

"Human divers often visit shipwrecks too."

"I thought humans couldn't breathe underwater," said Luna.

"They can't on their own, but they carry metal tanks on their back and breathe the air in through a mask," Rohan explained. "They usually stay fairly close to the surface, so you should be safe if you only go to the deeper wrecks."

"And watch out for sharks," warned Indra. "They generally leave merpeople alone, but the tiger sharks in the Red Sea can be particularly nasty. There are also quite a few giant moray eels there too. They might attack if you disturb them."

Coralie nudged Kai. "What did the baby eel say to his mummy when he saw a shark?" she muttered.

"What?' said Kai.

"Mummy, I'm *eel-ly* scared!" They both giggled while Naya, Luna and Marina groaned.

"OK, I think you're ready to go," said Indra, hastily shooing them away before Coralie could tell any more jokes.

The gang swam to the edge of the whirlpool. The white bubbles were foaming and frothing as it spun round and round. Coralie's heart sped up as she looked at the swirling water in front of her. Excitement fizzed from her head to her tail. This was it – they were going on another adventure!

"I'll go first," Marina said, "because I've—"

But Coralie didn't let her finish. "Red Sea, here we come!" she cried, diving into the whirlpool.

For a few wild moments, she spun round and round in a swirling cloud of white bubbles. She didn't know which way was up and which was down, but then the whirlpool flung her out into a warm turquoise sea.

Turning the right way up and looking around, she could see she was near the edge of a reef of colourful coral and giant sea fans. In the distance there was a carpet of pink, blue and gold anemones, their tentacles waving

in the gentle currents. Bright starfish clung
to grey rocks and shoals of small, bright fish
swept by while larger fish floated past more
slowly, their mouths opening and closing.

The others shot out of the whirlpool one
by one.

"We're here!" whooped Kai, grabbing hold
of Tommy's shell and letting the turtle pull
him through the clear blue water. "We're in
the Red Sea!"

"Why did you go first?" Marina said crossly to Coralie.

"You can't always be the one to go first," Coralie retorted.

They frowned at each other.

"It doesn't seem too scary here," said Luna, gazing around in relief. "Look, Melly, there's a dugong!" She pointed to where a large grey creature that looked very like Melly was grazing on seagrass. Melly swam over to touch noses and say hello.

"Ooh, a crown butterflyfish!" said Naya, spotting a thin silver fish with black stripes and a red tail nibbling at some algae. "They only live here in the Red Sea and a couple of other places in the world. I've always wanted to see one. This is *clam-tastic*!"

While Naya swam after the crown butterflyfish, Octavia propelled herself over to a cluster of rocks. She was about to grab hold of one when a black eel with white speckles on its body and sharp teeth lunged out of a crevice, snapping at her fiercely. Octavia darted out of the way just in time and shot back to the gang in a stream of bubbles.

"Oh, poor Octavia," said Naya, swimming over. "Did that eel frighten you?"

Octavia nodded and cuddled into her arms.

"We'd better be careful," said Marina. "Remember what Indra said. There are quite a few dangers in the Red Sea. Look, can you all see that stingray hiding in the sand?"

Coralie looked at where Marina was pointing. She could just make out the flat, mottled stingray, perfectly camouflaged on the sea floor.

"Be careful not to brush against the stinger on its tail!" warned Marina. "Now, which way should we go, I wonder? How about—"

"I think we should go this way!" said Coralie quickly, not wanting Marina to take charge. She swam towards where she could

see some deeper, darker blue water beyond
a cluster of black coral trees. "Follow me,
everyone!"

"Wait, Coralie!" Marina shouted.
"We should check for dangers first."

But Coralie didn't want to wait. "It's fine.
Come on!" she called, increasing her speed.

She swooped round the black coral trees
and then stopped dead as she came face to
face with a very large fish with silvery blue
scales and a yellow head and tail. It was
hovering protectively
over a patch of sand.
The first fin on
its back stiffened
when it saw
Coralie, and it
rolled slightly
on to its side,
glaring at her
with its large

eyes. Coralie started to feel nervous. It didn't look at all happy to see her.

"It's OK, fish, I'm not going to hurt you," she said soothingly. "I—"

She broke off with a yell as the fish lowered its head and charged at her, its strong jaws snapping!

Chapter Three
Under Attack!

Coralie yelped as the angry fish bit her on the arm. It shot away from her, heading towards its pile of sand. She swam backwards, waving her arms as the others came round the black coral. "Watch out!" she cried. "Stay back! There's an angry fish here."

The fish raced at the others and they scattered in different directions. "This way!" cried Coralie. "Quick!"

"No!" shrieked Marina as Coralie went to swim over the patch of sand the fish was guarding. She lunged at Coralie's tail and grabbed the fluke, stopping her in her tracks. "It's a titan triggerfish," she gasped as the fish chased Luna and Naya. "Her nest goes up in a cone shape from the seabed. If you try to go over it, you'll just swim through it and that'll make her even more furious." She pulled Coralie to the left. "We need to go this way instead. Come on, everyone! Follow me!"

They all hurried after Marina with the fish snapping angrily at their tails. Once they were safely away from her nest, the triggerfish let them go and swam back to guard her nest again. The gang didn't slow down though. They swam to where the water changed from turquoise to royal blue and finally came to a stop by some coral caves near the edge of the reef.

"Ow," said Coralie, examining her arm. The fish's teeth hadn't been very sharp, but there was a bruise forming.

"Here, I'll put some of my healing paste on it," said Naya, opening her bag and taking a tub out. She'd made the green paste inside from some plant leaves she'd found on their last adventure to an underground river in the jungle in Mexico.

"I think we need something to eat," said Kai, getting some seaweed biscuits out of his bag and handing them round.

Naya smoothed the paste on to Coralie's arm. "That should make it feel better."

"Thanks," Coralie said, feeling guilty. It was lucky none of her friends had been hurt. "I'm sorry about that fish attacking us."

"That's OK," said Kai, munching on a biscuit. "You couldn't have known it would be there."

"I did tell you not to go racing off, Coralie," Marina pointed out. "You haven't been to the Red Sea before, but I have. You should have listened to me."

Coralie felt guilty, and Marina telling her off didn't make her feel any better. "Just because you've been here before doesn't mean that we have to do everything you say, Marina," she said crossly. "Stop being so bossy."

Marina's face fell. "I'm not bossy," she said.

"Yes you are!" Coralie retorted. "You're the bossiest person I know!"

Luna quickly swam off to a bed of anemones. She didn't like it when people argued.

"I let you be the director of the play," Marina protested.

"You didn't *let* me," Coralie burst out. "It wasn't up to you. The play was my idea!"

"Oh, please stop arguing, you two!" Kai groaned. "You're ruining our adventure."

Naya suddenly shrieked loudly, "Luna! Be careful!"

Luna was swimming by a bed of pink anemones, watching three orange-and-white clownfish nosing happily between the fronds. For a moment, Coralie couldn't see why Naya sounded so alarmed, but then she spotted a tiger shark's menacing dark grey snout poking out of a nearby coral cave. Its beady black eyes were fixed on Luna. To Coralie's horror, it swam out of the cave, moving slowly from side to side. She knew it was what some sharks did just before they attacked.

Coralie and Marina both moved at the same time, charging through the water to get to Luna, but the shark was quicker than either of them. With a burst of speed, it shot like an arrow towards the younger mergirl. Luna stared at it in terror.

"Hum, Luna, hum!" shouted Marina. "Use your magic!" But Luna seemed to be frozen in fear.

Coralie heard Naya and Kai shout and then rocks and shells started flying past her head as her friends hurled them at the shark.

Hearing the noise, Melly, Dash, Octavia, Tommy and Sami raced over. They barrelled into the shark's side, but it was much stronger than them and it didn't even falter. Its mouth opened, revealing razor-sharp teeth...

Coralie swam as fast as she could and flung herself at its tail, grabbing hold. Marina was beside her in an instant. They both hung on tightly, their teeth gritted. Coralie felt a rush of intense relief that Marina was there with her.

"You are not getting Luna!" Marina panted.

"No way!" gasped Coralie.

With an angry snap of its jaws, the
shark pivoted round. The sudden spinning
movement loosened Coralie and Marina's grip
and, with a flick of its muscular tail, the shark
flung them away as if they weighed no more
than shrimps. Then it turned back to Luna.

Coralie righted herself and saw the shark
bearing down on her cousin again. It was
going to get her! "Luna!" she screamed.

Suddenly an enormous shape loomed out of
the blue water. It was at least six times bigger

than the shark. The creature had a dark grey back, a pale spotted belly and long pectoral fins that dangled underneath it. Its large knobbly head rammed into the shark's side, sending it flying through the water.

"A humpback whale!" Marina exhaled loudly as the shark shook itself, glared at the young whale and then swam away.

"They're… They're usually friendly, aren't they?" stammered Coralie as the creature swam up to Luna.

"This one is!" cried Luna, swimming forward and hugging its fin. "This is Wally, everyone!" The others watched in astonishment as the whale gently patted her back with its other fin. Its eyes were kind and gentle.

"Is that the whale your mum helped, Luna?" called Naya.

"Yes," said Luna, gently touching a scar on the creature's side. "He must have recognized me and come to help. Thank you, Wally!"

The whale opened his mouth and made
a gentle singing sound. Luna hummed back
and Wally sighed deeply. Coralie felt relief
wash over her. Thank goodness for the whale!
And thank goodness for Marina, she thought,
glancing at her friend. If they hadn't worked
as a team, the shark might have reached
Luna before Wally could come to the rescue.
She shot a grateful smile at Marina, but
Marina didn't meet her gaze.

"Wally, these are my friends," said Luna, beckoning everyone over.

Coralie grinned as she approached. "Hi, Wally, it's *whaley* nice to meet you!"

Naya groaned.

"What? I'm only giving him a nice *whale-come*!" said Coralie with a giggle. She automatically dodged away from Marina who usually flicked her with her tail when she made silly jokes. But Marina didn't even roll her eyes. Coralie was surprised. Was Marina still upset because of their argument?

The whale made a curious questioning sound, tilting its head slightly to one side as he looked at them.

"You're asking why we're here in the Red Sea, Wally?" Luna guessed. "It's because we want to explore a shipwreck. We want to find out more about humans."

Wally nodded for a moment and then slowly started to swim away.

"Oh, he's going," said Luna, disappointed.

Wally paused, then beckoned to them with one of his fins.

"I think he wants us to go with him," said Marina.

"Should we?" said Naya.

Marina opened her mouth and then paused. "What do you think, Coralie?" she asked.

Coralie blinked. She wasn't used to Marina asking her what they should do. "Me? Oh, um, I think... Yes we should!"

"Then let's go," said Marina, but she spoke more quietly than normal.

Wally flapped both of his long pectoral fins gently and looked at them as if he was hoping they would understand.

Dash shoved one of his own pectoral fins into Coralie's hand and then whistled at her, nodding at Wally. "You think Wally wants us to hold on to his fins, Dash?" Coralie said.

Dash nodded.

"OK, let's try that," said Coralie, wondering why the whale wanted them to.

They all swam over to his fins and held on. Coralie glanced at Marina who was tucking Sami carefully into her hair. She was still shocked that Marina had asked for her opinion. She remembered how Marina's face had fallen when Coralie had accused her of being bossy. She'd looked really hurt.

That was mean of me, Coralie thought. *I'd better say sorry.* She opened her mouth to apologize, but Wally flicked his huge tail fin and she didn't have a chance to speak before he was diving down into the depths.

"*Wheeee!*" cried Kai as the whale towed them along. Shoals of little fish rushed out of their way, swirling round the huge whale.

"Where's he taking us?" called Luna.

"I don't know!" answered Coralie as Wally flicked his tail and sped up. "But we'd better hang on tight!"

41

Chapter Four
The Shipwreck

Wally took them down to where the water was darker and colder and then stopped. Through the gloom, Coralie could just make out a giant shadowy shape nestling on the ocean floor. "It's an old ship!" she gasped.

"Oh, thank you, Wally!" cried Luna, letting go of the whale's fin and swimming up to stroke his face. "You must have understood what I said about us wanting to see a shipwreck. You're so clever!"

Wally looked pleased and he started to

sing softly to her, a haunting musical sound. Luna hummed along with him and the whale blinked happily.

"We need some light so we can see better," Naya said, opening her bag and taking out five lanterns made from glass jars. They contained bioluminescent algae and ground sea pansy as well as magic mermaid powder. When the merchildren shook the lanterns, the pouch with the algae liquid broke open and, as it mixed with the mermaid powder, the substances reacted and glowed, creating light. Naya handed the lights out and they all shook them hard. Bluey-green light sputtered out, weak at first, but getting stronger and stronger.

"Jumping jellyfish!" whispered Coralie, holding up her lantern. The shipwreck was an eerie, mysterious sight. It looked almost like the giant skeleton of some long-dead sea creature. The sails, ropes and most of the wooden deck planks had rotted away, but the hull and the railings round the deck were still in place. Rust was eating holes in the metal and everything had a thick, bumpy coating of grey, orange and yellow rust that had formed over many years.

Soft corals clung to the skeleton of the ship and covered the remaining deck. Triangular-shaped batfish with striped bodies and pale yellow tails were swimming in and out of the portholes while a shoal of large silver jackfish arched over the front of the ship. One of the thick wooden masts had broken off and was lying beside the ship. It was now covered with coral but the ship's other mast was still standing tall and proud, reaching high up into the deep blue water. At the base of it a single lionfish floated, waving its feathery fins and watching them warily.

"Awesome," said Kai. "We found a real shipwreck!"

"Thank you so much for bringing us here, Wally," called Luna.

Wally waved a fin at them and drifted away into the blue, his whale song echoing back.

"The wreck is almost like a mini coral reef," said Marina, swimming closer.

"The sea's transforming it," said Naya softly. "Turning it from a place where humans *used* to live to a place where sea creatures *can* live now."

"Let's explore but we should all stay

together," said Marina.

Coralie nodded. She'd learned her lesson
earlier. "Yes, we should do what Marina says."

Marina shot her a hurt look. Coralie's eyes
widened as she realized Marina must have
thought she was being sarcastic. "No, Marina,
I meant it!" Coralie started to protest, but
Marina was already swimming away with
Naya, heading up the metal side of the
hull towards the railing. Coralie sighed.

She wished they hadn't argued earlier.
They were usually really good friends.
When we're next alone, I'll definitely apologize,
she thought.

She, Kai and Luna followed Marina and
Naya up over the railings and across the deck
where there were old rusty winches and chains.
A speckled moray eel was nestled among
the chains. It opened its mouth in warning,
showing sharp teeth, as they quickly swam past.

A lot of the upper deck where the sailors
would once have stood and worked had rotted
away, leaving gaping holes. While Naya
and Marina stopped to inspect the ship's
large funnel, Coralie peered curiously down
through the gaps in the deck, looking into
the belly of the ship below. She could see the
remains of passageways, rooms and a rusting
spiral staircase that connected the different
levels of the ship, as well as all kinds of
strange human objects.

"I wonder what all those things are," Coralie said to Kai, pointing at them.

Just then, Tommy swam up to Kai and butted him with his head. "What is it?" Kai asked. Tommy urgently motioned upwards with a flipper.

"Look, Coralie," Kai said, raising his lantern and peering through a cloud of silver fish that were swirling around above them. "There's a length of netting caught on the mast and something's stuck in it!"

"It's a turtle," said Coralie as the fish swooped away into the sea. "Come on, let's free it."

"I'll come too!" said Luna.

The three of them swam upwards. The large piece of netting had caught on the top of the tall post where the sails had once hung and a young leatherback turtle was tangled in it. It twisted and turned, its flippers waggling in panic as it tried to free itself. Tommy swam up and nuzzled it as Luna started to hum. The turtle blinked, its dark little eyes flicking towards her. It stopped struggling. Still humming, Luna slowly swam

closer and stroked its head. It lay still as
she began to untangle its flippers and shell.
Kai and Coralie hung back slightly, not
wanting to risk scaring it while Luna worked
her magic. The turtle watched her trustingly.
Finally, it was free and Luna pulled the net
away, releasing the turtle. It kissed her cheek
with its stubby snout and then swam away
happily into the blue sea.

Naya and Marina had noticed what
was going on and swum up to join them.
"Well done, Luna!" called Marina.

Coralie hugged her cousin. "You're
completely brilliant or should I say *turtle-y*
brilliant!"

Luna started to pull the net off the mast.
"Horrible thing!" she said, glaring at it.
"I hate nets."

"Why hasn't it rotted away like the sails and
ropes?" Coralie asked, helping her.

Naya inspected the net. "It's a modern net,

made of plastic. It wouldn't have been on this boat, which is really quite old. It must have fallen down through the water more recently. It was probably from a big fishing boat."

"I hope it rots soon," said Kai.

"It won't," said Naya sadly. "These nets don't start to rot for hundreds of years. They just stay in the ocean, causing trouble."

They took the net off the mast. There was a lot of it and it was very heavy.

"What are we going to do with it? We can't just leave it here," said Kai.

"It weighs too much for us to carry around with us. Let's roll it up and put it some place where other sea creatures won't get caught up in it," said Marina.

They all helped roll the net up and then carried it down to the seabed. Marina and Naya buried it deep in the sand.

"I don't know how Marina can say human aren't dangerous," Coralie muttered to Kai and Luna. "Look at the stuff they put in the oceans – it does so much harm."

Luna shivered. "I hope I never meet a human."

Once the net was safely buried, they continued their exploration of the ship, heading further along the deck towards the bow. The coral grew even thicker here. A shoal of bright orange fish swooped past and another speckled eel twisted through the water as it swam down into the lower level of the wreck.

"I want to explore inside," said Coralie, watching the eel wriggle off into the inky blackness.

"But what if human divers come?" Luna said anxiously. "We won't be able to get away from them if we're inside the wreck."

"Indra said humans usually only dive to shallow wrecks and this one is pretty deep," Coralie pointed out, squeezing Luna's hand reassuringly. "I'm sure we'll be fine."

Naya used her lantern to peer down beneath the deck. "I think Coralie's right. The inside looks untouched. If this was somewhere humans visited, I think they'd have taken their objects back to the surface."

"We can't come all this way and not explore properly," Marina said.

"That would be such a shame," agreed Kai.

"And we still need to get some ideas for our play," said Coralie. "After all, that's what we came here for."

"What do you think, Luna?" Naya asked. "We'll only go inside if you're happy to come with us."

"It will be really good fun," said Coralie, looking hopefully at her cousin.

Luna smiled. "OK," she said. "It sounds like it's safe."

Marina beamed. "*Clam-tastic!* It's time for us to go wreck-diving then!"

Chapter Five
Exploring the Wreck

Coralie and Kai led the way as the friends
dived through the metal beams into the floor
immediately below the main deck. A huge
cloud of almost translucent glassfish enveloped
them, making it almost impossible to see, but
as the tiny fish swirled away the gang saw that
they were in a passage with gaping doorways
on either side. The doors had fallen off and
the remaining structure was heavily coated in
rust and algae. There were wooden panels that
must have once formed the walls, but were

now rotting on the floor.

Dash cuddled closer to Coralie. She stroked him, sensing he didn't like the strange, enclosed space with its reminders of human life. The other pets seemed just as wary. Sami buried himself in Marina's hair and Octavia hung on to Naya's arm, while Melly and Tommy stayed as close as they could to Luna and Kai.

Coralie looked curiously through the nearest doorway. Inside, she found a cooking range and the metal frame of a long table. There was a jumble of objects in the sand on the floor. "This looks like it might have been the room where the humans cooked," she said to Kai and Naya who had followed her in.

Naya picked up a plate and blinked in surprise at how heavy it was. "It's made of metal. Weird." The merpeople used old scallop shells as plates. "And their pots are made of metal too," she said, lifting one up.

"Not coral like ours."

Kai joined her and sifted through some more things on the floor. He held up two metal objects with prongs at one end. "Look, mini tridents!"

"They wouldn't be much good at fighting off sharks!" said Coralie.

"Oh wow! I've read about those things!" said Naya, her eyes lighting up. "They're called forks. Humans use them for eating." She picked one up from the floor and then pulled out her notebook and started sketching it. "I can't believe I'm actually holding a human fork!" she said in excitement.

Coralie examined a metal pot with a long handle on one side. "What do you think this is?" she said to Kai. She put it on her head.

"A hat that humans wear while they eat things with their forks?" "Or maybe they used it as a helmet when they had battles. Attack!" cried Kai, brandishing the forks in his hand. Coralie grabbed a metal plate and used it as a shield.

As they fought with the forks, Marina and Luna went to investigate a room on the other side of ship. "Hey, guys, there's a bedroom here and a … and a… Actually, I don't know what sort of room this is!" Marina called. "Come and see."

They joined her. There was a large room with round portholes in the wall and a big iron bed frame tipped up on its side. Panels had come away from the walls and were lying on the floor. Next to the bedroom was a smaller room with a large oval-shaped tub standing on curved feet at the far end. There was also a smaller rectangular tub standing high up on iron legs with a cracked mirror on the wall behind it. The walls and floor were covered with pale rectangles of thin, smooth stone.

"I think these are called tiles," said Naya, swimming up and touching the pale rectangles in fascination. Many were cracked and some had fallen off the wall and were lying smashed on the floor. "Humans put them on the floors in their houses and sometimes on the walls."

"Why?" said Kai.

"I don't know," Naya admitted.

"Maybe they play games with them," said Kai, turning upside down and walking on his hands, putting one on each tile.

"What's this thing for?" said Coralie, swimming over to the big tub. She got inside it. There were pointy metal objects at one end with handles at the top. She turned them and waited for something to happen, but nothing did. "What do these handles do?"

"They seem to connect to those tubes," said Naya, her eyes following the pipes on the wall. "Maybe water once came out of them?"

"But why would you fill a tub with water?" said Luna.

The gang exchanged mystified looks.

"Maybe it's where they wash their shoes," said Naya suddenly. "Humans have feet, not tails, and they wear shoes on their feet. This could be the place where they cleaned their shoes."

"Humans are so weird," said Kai.

The others all nodded in agreement.

"Can we go down to the lower level now? I want to find the engine room," said Naya. "Ships like this had masts and sails, but they were powered by steam engines. The cargo rooms will be down there too – that's where the goods the ships were transporting were kept. We might find some more interesting things." Her eyes gleamed. "Things that would give me inspiration for my inventions!"

They all swam down an encrusted spiral staircase that led deeper into the belly of the ship. It was even darker down here and they needed every scrap of light from their lanterns in order to see. At the bottom they found the entrance to the engine room.

"Oh, barnacles!" Naya gasped in delight,

swimming inside and gazing at the enormous metal engine with its network of pipes and tubes. Tiny silver and blue fish swooped around. The engine room reached all the way up to the top deck of the boat and had steps and ladders. Naya swam over to a workbench that still had some old tools and oil cans on it.

"Engines are boring," said Coralie.

"How can you say that?" said Naya, looking up at all the pipes. "This is amazing!"

"I'd rather find things like clothes humans wore or more of the things they ate with,' said Coralie.

"Maybe there'll be some stuff like that in the other rooms down here," said Marina. "We could go and have a look. If ... um ... you want to?" She gave Coralie a cautious look.

"Yes, definitely," said Coralie.

"Call if you need us, Naya," said Kai.

They swam through the shoals of darting fish. The corridor down here on the lower floor was narrower than on the floor above and they had to duck under the occasional fallen metal beams, but at last they reached two rooms. Marina and Luna turned into one, while Coralie and Kai went to explore the other.

Coralie's eyes grew wide as she took in the room. In the corners were lumps of black rock and there was a strange-looking human object in the middle. It had a big wheel with a large empty metal container shaped like an enormous metal shell sitting on top and two handles at the back. Coralie lifted the handles up. It was heavy but she realized that, if she pushed it, it trundled along the floor on its wheel.

"Look at this weird thing, Kai!" she said in delight.

"Cool! Give me a ride!" Kai dived into the container and clung to the sides as Coralie wheeled him around. She pushed him as fast as she could until the wheel caught on a stone causing the object to stop abruptly, throwing Kai out. He landed with his hands in the pile of black rocks.

When he pulled them out, they were covered in black gunk.

"Ew!" Coralie exclaimed.

"I'm the evil human wreck monster!" Kai dived at Coralie, reaching for her with his messy fingers. Coralie squealed and dodged away. She shrieked as Kai chased her round the room.

"Hey, everyone, come and look at this!" called Marina from the other room. "We've found something!"

Kai washed the gunk off his hands in the seawater and he and Coralie went to join Marina and Luna. The other room was vast! It had a giant hole in its side and it was now half full of sand. Marina was tugging at the handle of something that she had found buried in the sand. "Can you help me?" she called. "It's really heavy!"

They all grabbed hold and pulled as hard as they could until they had managed to drag out a large wooden chest.

"I wonder what's inside," said Marina.

"Treasure?" said Kai hopefully.

Coralie felt a rush of excitement. Could there really be treasure inside? Maybe gold coins or jewels?

"Let's take it upstairs and find out!" she exclaimed.

Chapter Six
Dressing Up

Luna raced to tell Naya what they had found while Marina, Coralie and Kai hauled the chest to the upper deck, to the kitchen, where they'd found the pots and forks. They tried to open it, but it was locked, and although the key was still in the lock it wouldn't turn.

"We can't get into it!" said Marina in frustration as she tried to turn the key.

"Hang on!" said Naya suddenly. "I've got an idea. Wait here."

She returned a few moments later with

an oilcan from the engine room. It had a long thin spout with a stopper at one end. Naya pulled out the stopper, slid the key from the lock and carefully trickled some oil into the keyhole before she put the key back in.

"Why hasn't this chest rotted like the other wooden things on the ship?" asked Luna, touching the grooved sides.

"The sand it was buried in would have protected it from the seawater," said Naya. She sat back. "OK, see if the key works now, Marina."

Marina took hold of the key and this time it turned! Marina and Naya heaved the lid open and everyone looked eagerly inside.

"Clothes!" said Marina. "Human clothes."

"I wanted it to be treasure," said Kai in disappointment.

"It might not be treasure, but it's fun to see what humans wear," said Marina. She pulled out the first item. It was a dress with a long, full skirt. Marina held it to her body and tail and twirled round.

Naya pulled out another dress and Coralie took out a pair of long thin things that were made of very fine material. "What are these?" she asked.

"I think they're called stockings. Humans put them on their legs," said Naya.

Coralie dangled them down in front of her tail and tried to imagine what it would be like to be human and have legs that you put "stockings" on instead of having a purple tail.

Octavia pulled some ribbons from the trunk and began to throw them in the air like streamers. Sami danced between them.

"What's this!" said Luna, taking something hairy out of the chest. "It's like a weird hat with hair on." She held it up so they could see what she had found. It seemed to be a thin cap with lots of hair attached. The hair was arranged in an elaborate bun at the back with three curly ringlets at each side.

"It's a wig!" Naya exclaimed. "Humans wear them on their heads."

Coralie put it on her head. The others giggled as she bobbed through the water, pretending to be human. "I am a human lady who fights sharks with my tiny trident that I call a fork!" she said, grabbing one from the side. "I have a special room with a big tub for washing my shoes and I wear a funny metal

hat on my wig." She plonked the pan she had found earlier on top of the wig.

The others all giggled.

"I'm going to wear a wig too!" said Kai. He took another one out of the trunk, a very elaborate tall white wig. "You can have one as well, Tommy!" He popped a wig of long blonde ringlets on to Tommy's head. The turtle blinked, his surprised dark eyes peeping out from under the curtain of curls.

Coralie poked Kai with the fork. "Fork chase!" she challenged. She shot away as Kai grabbed another fork and chased after her with a whoop. Dash and Tommy joined in.

Coralie dived through a serving hatch that led into the room next door and Kai followed. Their wigs flew off, landing on the thick layer of rubble coating the floor. The room was in a terrible state. The doorway to it was blocked by a panel of metal that had fallen from somewhere above and there was a gaping hole in the outside wall, hidden by a curtain of seaweed. The floor was covered in rotting panels of wood, sand and bits of broken furniture. Several large metal beams had come loose from the deck above. They slanted down across the room, their ends buried in the rubble.

As Coralie dodged between the beams, she suddenly came face to face with a huge bluey-green fish with big lips and worried eyes floating in the shadows. She screeched to a stop so suddenly that Kai bumped into her and they both flew sideways into one of the slanting beams. There was a creak and it wobbled precariously. For one horrible moment, Coralie thought that it was going to fall on them, but to her relief it stayed where it was.

"A humphead wrasse," breathed Kai, looking at the fish.

"Let's not disturb it – it must live here," said Coralie, swimming backwards away from the fish. Although it was as big as they were, Coralie and Kai weren't scared. Wrasse fish were gentle and usually very shy.

"I'm glad that beam didn't fall," said Kai. "This room isn't very safe, is it?"

Coralie looked around at the messy, sandy room. "It must have been damaged when the ship was wrecked," she said. As she looked at the hole in the side, she thought of a joke. "Hey, Kai, what do sea monsters like to eat?"

"What?" he said.

"Fish and ships!" she said with a grin.

Kai burst out laughing.

Just then, Marina poked her head through the serving hatch. "Hey, you two, come and look at what I just found in the chest!" Caught up in the excitement of exploring, she seemed to have forgotten about her argument with Coralie.

Coralie and Kai swam back through the hatch. "Look!" Marina said, showing them an ornament shaped like a mermaid.

"A mermaid! So humans do know about us

after all," said Coralie in surprise.

"My dad said there are stories about us, but humans don't think we're real," said Marina.

"Maybe that's what we should do our play about," said Coralie thoughtfully. "We could wear human clothes and wigs and pretend to be humans on a ship seeing merpeople for the first time. We could act out the humans spotting the merpeople and then attacking them—"

"Or we could show them seeing us and trying to be our friends," Marina put in. "I think that would be a better play."

"But humans wouldn't want to be friends. They'd just want to capture us like they catch whales and dolphins," argued Coralie.

"Do you think if a human saw us they'd shoot us with a harpoon, like they did to Wally?" said Luna, her eyes wide.

"I bet they would," said Coralie.

"No they wouldn't," said Marina, frowning.

"I think—"

"Guys!" Naya's voice cut across their argument. Hearing a note of fear in her voice, they swung round. Naya was looking out of one of the portholes. "I think we might be about to find out!" She pointed outside. "There are humans, and they're coming to the wreck!"

Their argument forgotten, Coralie and Marina exchanged horrified glances and raced to the porthole. Naya was right! Four humans in black diving suits with metal tanks on their backs and torches in their hands were swimming down towards them.

Chapter Seven
Danger!

The humans' powerful torch beams swept from side to side as they approached the old ship. All four divers had masks, mouthpieces with tubes that led to the tanks on their backs and large yellow-and-black fins on their feet. Streams of bubbles floated away from them as they breathed the air in the tanks.

"Dim your lanterns, everyone!" hissed Marina. "If they see our lights, they'll come inside."

Once the chemical reaction inside the

lanterns started, it couldn't be stopped, but Naya and Octavia had knitted seaweed covers that could block out the light. They all quickly pulled the covers down.

"What are we going to do?" said Coralie as they huddled together in the darkness and watched the divers getting closer.

"I don't like this, Coralie," said Luna, close to tears. "What if the humans see us?"

Coralie put an arm round her shoulders and hugged her. "It'll be OK," she whispered, hoping that was true.

"We'll look after you," said Marina, squeezing Luna's hand.

"Look! They're holding things! Do you think they're weapons?" Kai asked nervously.

One diver was unfolding a large square frame criss-crossed with a mesh of fine wires. Another was holding a rectangular black box with handles on both sides, and one of the others was carrying a long tube.

Coralie suddenly panicked – what if it *was* a weapon? "We've got to get out of here!"

"We can't. If we leave the ship now, they'll scc us," Marina hissed.

"But if they come into the ship they'll find us!" said Coralie, starting to move. "We have to hide, Marina."

"No, wait!" Marina said, grabbing her arm. "Let's watch for now and see what they do. If they look like they're going to come inside the ship, then we can hide."

"They seem to have stopped out there," whispered Naya. "They're looking at all the fish and coral."

"If they start trying to hurt any of the creatures here, I'll hurt them!" said Luna, sounding suddenly very fierce. "I don't care if I get harpooned!"

"What are they doing?" said Kai, frowning.

They watched as the divers spread out across the sand. The one holding the frame tossed it to the seafloor. She peered inside it and started making notes with a pen on a white board she had slung over her body. All the divers had similar boards attached to them by straps. Their torches were also connected to their wrists so that they could let go of them without them floating away.

"That diver over there is writing things down," said Naya, leaning forward curiously. "I wonder why."

"I think that one's got a weapon!" hissed

Coralie. She tensed as the diver she was watching laid the tube on the floor and opened it up. "Oh," she said in surprise as she saw that the case was full of science equipment.

The diver took out some little glass cylinders and started filling them with samples of sand from around the boat. Another diver got out a tape measure and began to measure some branching red coral that was growing on the fallen mast.

"They don't seem to be doing anything too dangerous," whispered Kai as the fourth diver pointed the little black box around and started clicking a button on the top. "Though maybe something's about to come out of that box."

"No! It's something humans call a camera," whispered Naya excitedly. "It can take pictures. I've always wanted to see how they work!"

"The humans don't seem to be capturing or hurting anything, do they?" said Luna slowly.

"It looks like they're just gathering

information," said Naya. "Like our scientists do."

The divers moved carefully and slowly, as if they were trying not to disturb anything. The young leatherback turtle that had been caught in the net earlier came gliding down through the water. One of the divers spotted it and nudged another. They smiled and watched it swim on its way as the one with the camera took pictures. Then one of the divers spotted an old plastic bottle that was lying on the ocean floor. Shaking his head, he put it into a bag slung round his waist.

"They're collecting litter," said Luna.

"They *do* care about the ocean," breathed Coralie.

Marina shot her a smile. "I told you. Lots of humans care. There are human organizations that try and protect the oceans, and lots of scientists who do underwater research, like my dad does."

"So these humans, the nice ones, they're really just like us?" said Luna.

"Yes, only they have to go to the surface to breathe when the air in their tanks runs out," said Naya.

"And they have legs instead of tails," said Kai. "And huge, long, flappy feet."

"Those aren't their real feet, barnacle brain," said Naya, grinning. "They're wearing things on their feet to help them swim!"

"Oh," said Kai, his eyes widening in surprise.

"They're coming closer," said Coralie
uneasily as the humans started to swim
towards the ship. "If they shine their torches
into this window, they'll see us."

Marina nodded. "Maybe it's time we hid."

But just then there was an echoing sound
that stopped the divers in their tracks. It was
a humpback whale singing! The divers swung
round. A huge grey shape with a knobbly head
loomed out of the blue depths.

"Wally!" said Luna.

With a slow flick of his tail and a waggle
of one of his fins, Wally turned so he was
cruising alongside the ship, swimming so
close to the divers they could almost reach
out and touch him. Coralie saw the divers'
delighted expressions. Wally sang again and
drifted away. Beckoning excitedly to one
another, the divers started to follow him, the
one with the camera taking photos and the
others scribbling notes.

"He's leading them away," Marina said.
"He must have realized we were trapped in
here and couldn't get out."

"Clever Wally!" Luna said, her eyes shining.

The gang watched in relieved silence as the
divers swam away. But then the diver at the
back of the group glanced over her shoulder
towards the wreck. At the exact same moment,
the large humphead wrasse fish decided to
swim out through the curtain of seaweed that
hid the hole in the hull of the boat.

The diver turned round to watch the fish.
Spotting the diver, the wrasse hastily swam
back through the seaweed into the safety
of the ship. The diver glanced at Wally
and the other humans, then back at the ship.
It looked like she couldn't decide what to
do, but suddenly she started swimming back
towards the wreck.

"Barnacles! She's following the wrasse into
the ship," Marina hissed.

"Quick! Time to hide!" Coralie said. "Let's go to the lower deck. She might not come down there."

"Octavia, why don't you and the other pets watch and check none of the other divers come back?" said Naya. "You can come and get us when the coast is clear."

Octavia nodded hard and waved her arms at Naya, urging her to go.

Coralie zoomed out of the kitchen with the others following. But, as they made their way to the depths of the ship, a loud crash came from the room with the blocked doorway. For a moment, the whole ship seemed to shake. They all stopped.

"What was that?" Naya said in alarm.

Coralie's eyes leaped to Kai's. "The beam!" they exclaimed. The unstable metal beam they had knocked into earlier must have finally fallen.

"Come on," urged Marina.

"No, wait!" said Coralie, her stomach swirling anxiously. She swam to the metal sheet covering the doorway and saw a small hole. She pressed her eye to it and caught her breath, her heart plummeting. The heavy metal beam had fallen down. The diver must have knocked it and now she was trapped beneath it! She was trying to push it off, but she clearly wasn't strong enough to move it.

"Oh no, no, no, no," Coralie whispered, shaking her head.

"What is it?" said Naya.

Coralie beckoned them over. One by one they peeped through the hole.

"That poor diver!" cried Luna in dismay.

"What are we going to do?" asked Naya.

"We have to help her," said Marina.

"But then she'll see us," Kai pointed out.

"Maybe her friends will realize she's missing and come back and find her," said Coralie hopefully.

"The air in her tank might run out before they find her," said Naya. "Humans can only breathe underwater when those tanks are full of air. If her air runs out, she'll die."

"We have to go in there," said Luna, heading for the kitchen doorway.

"Luna! Wait!" exclaimed Kai.

"No," Luna called over her shoulder. Her chin jutted out determinedly. "We can't let her die!"

"Luna's right," said Coralie, charging after her cousin. "We can't!"

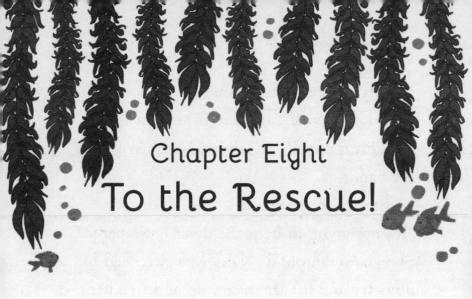

Chapter Eight
To the Rescue!

They all raced back into the kitchen and swam through the serving hatch. The diver was now lying still, her eyes closed. She had a wound on her forehead.

"Is she... Is she..." Luna quavered.

"No, she's not dead," whispered Naya. "Look at the bubbles around her and listen to the hissing noise the tank is making. That means she's still breathing."

"What are we going to do?" said Coralie, feeling panicky as she looked at the injured diver lying under the beam.

"I don't know," said Kai, his eyes wide.

"This is awful!' exclaimed Naya, wringing her hands.

"Stay calm, everyone," said Marina. "It's not going to help the diver if we panic." She glanced around. "OK, what we need to do is try and lift the beam up and free her. Coralie and Kai, why don't you grab that end over there? Naya, Luna, you help me with this end."

They all got into their positions and Marina counted them down. "OK. One... Two... Three... And LIFT!"

Everyone's arms strained as they tried to heave the heavy beam off the diver. It moved a few centimetres. The diver's eyes flickered open and then widened as she saw them. A look of disbelief flashed across her face before she groaned and shut her eyes again.

"She probably thinks she's imagining us!" Naya hissed.

"Keep lifting!" panted Marina. But try as they might they couldn't get the beam any higher.

"It's not working!" said Kai in frustration. "We're just not strong enough."

"Maybe we could go and find the other humans and bring them back here," Luna suggested.

"But then they'd all see us," said Marina. "If one person sees us, it's not too bad – the other people might not believe them – but if more than one person sees us then they'll have proof we're definitely real, especially if they take a picture of us with their camera. No, there has to be something else we can do."

Coralie turned to Naya, who had her thinking face on. "If we all lifted just one end of the beam, I think we could get it high enough to balance it on something, then we could lift the other end off the diver." She frowned. "But, for that to work, we need to find something strong that we can push easily under the beam."

The gang looked around, trying to see if there was anything they could use. Coralie kept thinking about what Naya had said. The word 'push' made her think of something... Then a picture popped into Coralie's mind and she finally remembered.

"I know what we can use!" she gasped. "Kai, come with me!" She raced out of the room.

"Where are we going?" Kai shouted, following her.

"To get that wheely thing we saw earlier!" said Coralie. "It's made of metal. It's strong and it can be pushed easily. We can use it for Naya's plan!" She shouted to their pets who were still keeping watch. "Dash! Tommy! We need you."

Dash and Tommy came swimming eagerly towards them.

Flicking her tail at double speed, Coralie led the way quickly down to the lower level. The wheely thing was heavy when it wasn't being pushed on its wheel, but she and Kai just managed to lift it with Tommy and Dash's help. "I hope we can get it up to where the diver's trapped," said Coralie, thinking anxiously of the twisting narrow passageways they had to swim up to get back to the upper level. She wasn't sure they would all fit.

"Even if we do get it up there, it's too big to fit through the serving hatch," said Kai, his shoulders sagging. "This isn't going to work, Coralie."

Coralie thoughts raced. There had to be some way round the problem. "How about we take it out through the hole in the room where we found the chest. We can then swim up the side of the ship with it until we get to the other hole, the one that leads into the room where the diver is. If we do that, we don't have to go through the hatch."

Kai whooped. "That's a great idea!"

Coralie grinned. "I think you mean it's a *wheely* good one!"

He high-fived her and then, with Dash and Tommy's help, they managed to push the heavy object out of the ship and carry it up through the water to the room where the diver was trapped. They burst through the curtain of seaweed. "Ta-da!" said Coralie.

Naya's face lit up. "A wheelbarrow! That's exactly what we need, Coralie!"

Sami, Octavia and Melly had joined the rest of the gang. Melly clapped her flippers while Sami bobbed up and down and Octavia danced in delight.

"A *wheelbarrow*," said Coralie, trying out the unfamiliar word and looking at Naya to check she'd said it right.

Naya nodded and swam over. "Humans use them for moving things around. It must have been for taking the coal into the engine room. Wow!" She stroked it as if it was an animal. "This is perfect, Coralie."

Marina beamed at Coralie. "Well done!"

Coralie was delighted.

"We need to hurry," Luna called, breaking off from humming to the diver. She was crouched down beside the injured human, stroking her face as if she was a trapped animal. The diver was staring at her, wide-eyed. She looked as if she couldn't believe what she was seeing. However, Luna's humming was keeping her calm. It seemed like Luna's magic didn't just work on sea creatures but on humans too!

Marina took charge again. "Right, everyone, get ready to try to lift this end. Pets, we'll need you to help too. Luna, you stay with the diver and, when we get the beam high enough, push the thing Coralie and Kai found under it. OK?"

They all gathered at one end, took hold of the beam and lifted. As the beam moved upwards, Tommy, Dash and Melly swam underneath and pushed with their backs, lifting it even higher.

"Now, Luna!" gasped Marina.

Luna left the diver and pushed the wheelbarrow underneath the beam.

"Set the beam down!" panted Marina. "But carefully."

They lowered it until the end was resting across the metal frame of the wheelbarrow.

"Now we need to lift the other end!" cried Marina.

They all raced to the other side.

The diver seemed to realize what they were

doing and, as the gang lifted the beam, she wriggled out from under it and slowly sat up, clutching her head.

Coralie felt a rush of relief that the diver didn't seem too badly injured. The wreckage and sand on the floor must have provided a thick, soft layer that she had sunk into when the beam had fallen on her. There was just the cut on her head. The diver put her fingers to it and blinked dazedly.

"Here," said Naya, swimming over. She took the healing paste out of her bag and gently smoothed some on to the diver's wound. "This will help."

"I've got snacks," said Kai, taking a few seaweed biscuits out of his bag. He held one out to the diver. She stared at it.

"Here. Eat it," said Kai, speaking slowly as if he was talking to a very young merchild. "Like this." He took a bite. "Yum-yum!" he said, rubbing his tummy. He held it out again.

The diver took it but held it up to her mask
and shrugged with a smile.

"She can't eat it because that would mean
taking off her breathing apparatus," Naya
realized.

Coralie couldn't imagine what it must be
like not to be able to eat and talk and breathe
underwater. Poor humans, they were really
missing out!

Naya's healing paste was starting to work.

The wound had stopped bleeding. Looking brighter, the diver pulled the underwater notepad from over her shoulder and drew a question mark with her pen, then held it up so they could see it. She pointed at them.

"I think she wants to know what we are," said Naya.

"We're merpeople," Luna said to the diver. "We look after the oceans." The diver frowned, not seeming to understand their language.

Octavia lay down, pretending to be injured, holding one arm dramatically to her face and thrashing about. Naya gently lifted her up and inspected her. "We look after sea creatures," she said to the diver.

"And we rescue them too," said Kai, still speaking very loudly as if that would somehow help the diver understand. He lifted up a piece of rotting wood and beckoned to Tommy. Tommy hid underneath it and Kai made a big show of lifting it up and then checking

Tommy to see if he was OK.

"We clear things up too," said Marina, darting round the room and stacking bits of wreckage neatly to demonstrate what she meant.

"And do research," said Naya. She pulled her own notebook out of her bag and swam around, looking at things and pretending to write notes. Then she took a tube out of her bag and mimed putting a sample of coral in it.

The diver smiled and took a tube out of her own bag attached to a belt round her waist. Then she pointed to the badge on the chest of her wetsuit.

"I think she's saying that's what she does too," said Marina.

"I know. We saw you," Luna said, smiling back. "You're just like us but with legs and feet, and you can't breathe underwater of course."

The diver looked round at the curtain of seaweed. She pointed to herself and then to the hole in the side of the ship.

"I think she's saying she's going to go," said Coralie.

The diver swam towards the hole and beckoned to them eagerly. She clearly wanted them to go with her. They all shook their heads.

"I wish we could make her understand she can't tell anyone," Marina said anxiously.

The diver pushed the curtain of seaweed back and Coralie felt a jolt of shock as she saw the other three divers heading towards the ship, the beams of their torches sweeping around.

"Her friends are here!" said Kai in alarm.

The diver beckoned to them again. When the gang all shook their heads, she looked disappointed. With a wave, she swam out.

They raced to the curtain and peeped through the fronds of seaweed. The diver's friends spotted her and swam swiftly to meet her.

"She's going to tell them about us!" said Coralie, her stomach churning.

The diver they had helped turned and pointed excitedly back to the ship, but the others seemed more concerned about the wound on her forehead. Pulling her board and pen round, she drew a picture and showed it to them.

Coralie caught her breath. It was a picture of a mermaid! She tensed, sure the other divers would come rushing into the ship to find them, but to her surprise they didn't. Two of them smiled through their masks while the third shook his head and inspected the diver's wound again.

"They don't believe her," Marina sighed in relief. "I told you – humans don't think we're real."

The diver looked frustrated. She started to swim back towards the ship, beckoning frantically. The other three looked at each other and then shrugged and followed her.

"They're all coming into the ship!" said Luna.

"What are we going to do?" said Kai.

"Think, think, think," Marina said to herself.

Coralie's eyes swept round the room and fell on the three wigs that she and Kai had been playing with earlier. "I've got it!" she exclaimed, grabbing one from the floor. "Quick, Dash, come here!"

Chapter Nine
Coralie Saves the Day

The four divers stopped and stared in astonishment as Dash swam out through the seaweed curtain with the long blonde wig balanced on his head. The one with the camera quickly started to take pictures. Dash's eyes sparkled as he looked out from under the wig and clapped his fins. Coralie could tell he was enjoying himself as he waggled his tail like a mermaid and bobbed over to the injured diver.

The other divers started to smile.

One of them picked up their slate, drew a quick mermaid shape with a line through it and then drew a dolphin with a wig instead. Then he pointed to the wound on his friend's head and mimed being hit on the head and feeling dizzy.

"They think that when she hit her head she mistook Dash for a mermaid," said Marina. She hugged Coralie. "Oh wow! This really was your best idea ever, Coralie!"

Coralie glowed. She was delighted that Marina seemed to have forgotten their argument and really pleased they'd helped the diver without being found out. It would have been awful if they'd been seen by any other humans and the merpeople's secret had got out.

The diver they had helped turned to swim back to the wreck, but her companions gently took hold of her arms and steered her away, shaking their heads.

"You saved the day, Coralie," said Luna as the injured diver took one last look in their direction, before giving in and following her friends back towards the surface.

"I didn't. Dash did!" said Coralie, grinning as the dolphin came swishing back to them. He bobbed round Coralie, pretending to bow, while everyone clapped and cheered him.

"You were a perfect mermaid, Dash!" Coralie told him, kissing him on the snout. "I'll have to give you a starring role in the play."

Dash whistled, looking very pleased with himself.

Octavia was not at all happy that Dash was getting so

much attention. She sneaked up and grabbed the wig from Dash's head, then put it on her own head. She danced away, waving her arms triumphantly, the ringlets hanging down like extra arms. Dash raced after her to get it back.

"Stop it, you two!" cried Naya. "You'll knock over more beams if you're not careful."

Octavia zoomed in front of Coralie and pointed to herself pleadingly with all eight arms.

"Yes, you can have a part in the play too, Octavia!" said Coralie with a grin. "All of you can," she added as Melly, Sami and Tommy looked hopefully at her too.

"But what is the play going to be about?" said Kai. "We still haven't decided."

Coralie looked thoughtful. "Well, this adventure has given me lots of ideas," she said. She had an idea now what the play would be about, but she wanted some time to think about it before she shared her plans with the others. "Do you think we can take the wigs and clothes home with us?" she asked.

Naya shook her head. "No. I don't think we should. They belong here on the wreck. We're not supposed to disturb marine environments and, though the things are human, they belong to the sea now."

Coralie sighed. "I guess so, but it's a pity. They'd have been useful, but we can always make our own costumes and props when we're back home on the reef."

"That sounds like fun," said Luna.

"Talking about the reef, we should be getting back," said Kai suddenly. "We've been down here for ages and it's going to take us longer to swim back to the whirlpool without Wally. Mum will be as mad as a tiger shark if she has to come and find us!"

None of them liked the idea of being told off by Indra so, after checking the humans had definitely gone, they swam out of the wreck.

"It's been a *spray-mazing* adventure!" said
Naya.

Coralie grinned. "It has, although at times
I was ... *a nervous wreck!*"

Even Kai groaned and splashed at her for
that one.

Coralie giggled and zoomed away in the
direction of the whirlpool. A few minutes later,
Marina caught up with her. "So, what ideas

have you got for the play?" she asked curiously.

Coralie tapped her nose mysteriously.
"I'm not telling till tomorrow."

"Well, whatever it is, I bet it'll be something amazing. You always have great ideas," Marina said. "I don't know what we'd have done if you hadn't thought of using the wheelbarrow to balance the beam or got Dash to convince the divers that their friend had seen a dolphin, not a mermaid – that was brilliant."

Marina's smile was so genuine that Coralie felt awful about hurting her feelings earlier. She realized she'd been so caught up with everything that had been happening that she still hadn't apologized. She wished she hadn't upset her friend. Marina could be bossy at times, but she was also brave, brilliant in a crisis and one of the most fun people Coralie had ever met.

"I'm really sorry about earlier, Marina!" she said, the words coming out in a rush.

"I shouldn't have called you bossy. You were amazing today when we were all panicking. You took control and got us working together. You were also right when you told me not to go dashing off when we first got here *and* you were right about humans too. I should have listened."

"It's OK," Marina said awkwardly. "I'm sorry that I'm bossy. I don't mean to be. I'm just used to taking charge. Before I came to live at Mermaids Rock, it was just me, Sami and Dad, and Sami likes it when I decide what we're going to do." The little seahorse peeped out from her hair and nodded in agreement. "My dad too," Marina went on. "You know what he's like – he's so into his research he'd forget to eat and sleep if I didn't remind him." She bit her lip. "But I'll try to be different if it annoys you. I love being friends with you and I'd hate it if you decided you didn't want to be my friend any more."

Coralie gave her a gentle shove. "Like that's ever going to happen! Don't change. We've had so much fun since you came to live at Mermaids Rock. I didn't mean what I said. I like you just the way you are."

Marina sighed in relief. "We do make a pretty good team, don't we?" she said, linking arms with her.

Coralie grinned. "Those tiger sharks better watch out!"

"Def-*FIN*-itely," said Marina, grinning.

Coralie looked at her indignantly. "Hey! I do the jokes."

"Sorry," said Marina with a smile. "Go on,

tell me one then."

Coralie never needed any encouragement. "Knock, knock."

"Who's there?" said Marina.

"Wally!" cried Luna from behind them.

Coralie glanced round at her in surprise. "That's not the answer, Luna."

"No – Wally!" Luna said, pointing. "Look! He's there, in front of you!"

The giant grey whale loomed out of the water and waggled his long fins.

"He's come to help us get to the whirlpool," said Luna.

"Hooray! With Wally helping, we might actually have a chance of getting back before Mum comes to find us!" said Kai.

They all grabbed hold of Wally's fins.

"Go, Wally, go!" cried Luna.

With a downward flick of his tail, Wally powered away, speeding easily through the blue water. Coralie whooped with delight as the Red Sea rushed by in a blur of blue. She'd made up with Marina, they'd had a *fin-credible* adventure and now she couldn't wait to go home to get started on their play!

Chapter Ten
Showtime!

"There you are!" said Indra, looking relieved as they shot out of the whirlpool at Mermaids Rock. "I was just about to come and find you. Are you all OK?"

"We're fine," said Kai, hugging her. "Thanks for letting us use the whirlpool, Mum."

"So, you didn't meet anything dangerous or get into any scrapes?" Indra asked anxiously.

"Oh no," they all said together, shaking their heads firmly.

"We found out lots about humans for our play," said Coralie.

"I'm really looking forward to watching it," said Indra. "What's it going to be about?"

"That's what we'd all like to know," Marina said, nudging Coralie.

"You'll find out soon," said Coralie mysteriously. "Thanks for the inspiration, guys! See you tomorrow!" She waved and swam away with Dash.

Her mind was buzzing with ideas and, although she was tired, after she'd had some food with her parents, she stayed up in her bedroom, writing a script.

"Done!" she finally said at midnight as she closed her notebook and sat back with a feeling of satisfaction. The play was sorted. Now she just needed to tell her friends!

The gang worked super hard all week, rehearsing, making costumes and wigs and scenery, until, at last, it was the day of the performance. Their parents gathered round the flat coral area they were using as a stage. There were other people there too: schoolfriends, some of the guards and even Sylvie, their teacher.

"This is it," Coralie said as they all got ready backstage. "Remember your lines, everyone!"

Naya had constructed a frame with seaweed curtains and had made a stage out of table coral. She didn't want to act so was organizing everything backstage. "OK, are you ready?" she hissed as the others got into their positions for the start. "Three, two, one and … curtain up!"

She pulled the lever opening the curtains and the play began. The first scene showed a group of merpeople – Coralie, Kai, Luna and Marina – rescuing and helping sea creatures. Octavia pretended to be caught in rubbish, her arms thrashing dramatically as they freed her from a net, and then Dash swam across the stage, one of his fins dangling limply and needing to be bandaged.

Then, after a quick costume change, the curtains opened again and they were all dressed as humans on a boat. Tommy was the captain, wearing a little hat and steering the ship, while Marina and Kai pranced about in dresses and wigs made of seaweed, pretending to eat food with tiny forks. Dash, Octavia and Melly were the ship's crew, hoisting sails and scrubbing the decks, until Naya made a loud crashing noise offstage and they all flung themselves around, crying and yelling as they acted out the ship being wrecked.

"Person overboard!" shouted Marina.

"Our ship's breaking up!" yelled Kai.

"Oh no, we're all going to die!" Coralie screamed.

"Wait! What's that?" shouted Marina, pointing offstage. "Could something be coming to our rescue?"

Dash and Tommy had swum offstage, but returned dressed up in a humpback whale costume. Dash was the head of the whale and Tommy was the tail. They were supposed to help Luna and Octavia rescue the humans from the shipwreck, but they started having an argument as to which way they should go first. Tommy pulled one way and Dash pulled the other until the whale costume split in half, leaving them both looking rather surprised in the middle of the stage. The audience roared with laughter and clapped.

Naya swam on and hastily mended the costume while Octavia entertained the audience by dancing round the stage in a wig.

Finally, the play restarted and Luna, Octavia, Dash and Tommy acted out how the mermaid, the whale and the octopus came to the rescue, carrying the humans – Coralie, Kai and Marina – safely up to the surface.

"We promise that from now on we'll be sensible and look after the seas," cried Marina, waving. "Thank you, little mermaid and your wonderful friends!"

"And so our story ends," said Coralie to the audience. "From that day onwards, the humans did all they could to find out more about the oceans, keep the seas clean and help marine creatures. And the merpeople did the same. They all worked together and made the world a better place!"

As the audience clapped and cheered, the gang and their pets bowed over and over again until Naya finally pulled the curtains across the stage.

"That was awesome!" exclaimed Marina, hugging Coralie as their pets danced round them.

"The audience really loved it!" said Coralie

happily. "Did you hear all the clapping?"

Naya rushed on to the stage to join them. "That was really fun and we learned so much!"

"I want to do another play," said Luna.

"I want another adventure!" said Kai.

"Where do you think we should go next?" asked Marina eagerly. "How about the Irish Sea? Or the Atlantic Ocean?"

"Or a mangrove swamp?" suggested Kai.

"I'd like to go and see some penguins," said Luna.

"Just think, there's a whole huge world out there waiting for us," said Marina, swinging Coralie round.

Coralie felt joy burst through her. Marina was right. The world was an amazing place and they had only just begun to explore it. There was so much more for them to see. So many more creatures for them to meet and – best of all – so many more exciting adventures for them to have!

Turn the page to learn more about the Red Sea and the creatures that live there!

THE RED SEA

The Red Sea – an inlet of the Indian Ocean –
can be found between Asia and Africa.
It's bordered by a number of countries.
On the eastern shore, there's Jordan, Israel,
Saudi Arabia and Yemen. On the western shore,
there's Egypt, Sudan, Eritrea and Djibouti.

The Red Sea is 1,400 miles long and 221
miles wide, at its widest point.

You can find more that 1,200 species of fish
in the Red Ocean. That includes forty-four
species of sharks. Unsurprisingly, the Red Sea
is a top site for divers!

The Red Sea is also home to the world's fastest
fish – the solitary sailfish! It can swim at up to
68 miles per hour.

The Red Sea's coral reef ecosystem stretches for 1,240 miles along the coastline. Some parts of these reefs are up to 7,000 years old!

Divers don't only come to see the amazing biodiversity, there are remnants of ships, tugboats and tankers. Divers can learn about the sea's history through these wrecks.

There are many theories behind how the Red Sea got its name. One claims that it gets its name from the changes in colour that are observed in the water. Usually it's a strong blue-green, but sometimes the sea is full of an algae, which turns the sea a reddish colour when it dies off.

MEET WALLY
THE HUMPBACK WHALE

Humpback whales can be found in every
ocean in the world. They have light bellies
and dark backs, and a small hump in front of
their dorsal fin, which is why they're called
"humpback". Each whale has a unique fluke
(tail), which can be used to identify them.

They have a massive tail fin, which they
use to propel themselves through the water.
Sometimes they even propel themselves out
of the water! When wales leap from the water
and then land with a huge splash, this is
called breaching. Scientists believe that whales
breach in order to knock pests off their bodies.
But they could be doing it for fun!

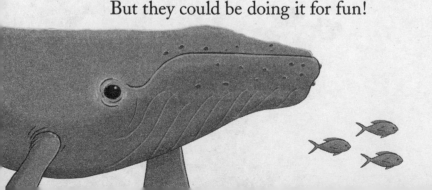

Humpback whales are "famous" for the long and complex songs they sing. These can last up to thirty minutes and can travel amazing distances through the oceans! The male whales "sing" to attract females, or to alert other males that they're in the area, and can create new songs every season.

Humpback whales can be found near coastlines, where they feed on plankton, krill and small fish. Every year, the whales migrate from their summer feeding grounds, near the poles, to warmer winter breeding waters closer to the Equator.

The number of humpback whales was reduced, before a ban on commercial whaling was introduced in 1985. Since then the population size has increased. The biggest threats they face today are collisions with ships and becoming tangled in fishing gear.

Collect them all and dive into Mermaids Rock!

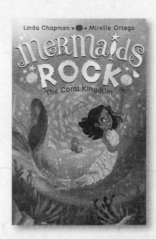

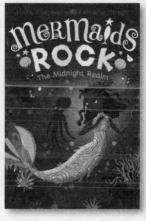

About the Author

Linda Chapman is the best-selling
author of over 200 books. The biggest
compliment Linda can receive is for a
child to tell her they became a reader
after reading one of her books.
Linda lives in a cottage with a tower in
Leicestershire with her husband, three
children, three dogs and two ponies.
When she's not writing, Linda likes to
ride, read and visit schools and libraries
to talk to people about writing.

www.lindachapmanauthor.co.uk

About the Illustrator

Mirelle Ortega is a Mexican artist
based in Los Angeles. She has a
MFA in Visual Development from
the Academy of Art University in San
Francisco. Mirelle loves magic, vibrant
colours and ghost stories. But more
than anything, she loves telling unique
stories with funny characters and a
touch of magical realism.

www.mirelleortega.com